This book belongs to

Dedicated to my grandchildren
Oliver, Nathan and Landon

Zep the Alien

And his adventures

Written and illustrated by J.K. Meadows

There was a little Martian
named Zep.
Zep lived on Mars, where
everthing was red and rocky .

Zep was always curious...

One day, while playing with his flying saucer, Zep flew too close to Earth and lost control of his ship.

Zep crashed landed on a farm and found himself in a very different world.
CRASH!

The ground was green, the sky was blue, and there where animals everywhere!

Zep was so amazed of
the beauty of this
strange, new world.

At first, Zep was scared.
He had never seen
anything
Like this before.

Then he noticed that the animals on the farm were very friendly.

They wagged their tails
WOOOOF! WOOOOF!

And even chased each other around.

They even mooed.
Zep couldn't help but giggle
at their silly behavior.
MOOOO

As Zep explored the farm.

He met three little boys named, Oliver, Nathan and baby Landon. The three boys were very excited And fascinated by Zep and his flying saucer.

The boys wanted to know all about where Zep came from and what he was doing on their farm . Zep told the boys all about Mars and how he crashed on Earth.

Oliver, Nathan and baby Landon
offered to help Zep fix his flying
saucer so he could go back home.
Zep was very grateful!

Together Oliver, Nathan, baby Landon and Zep, set out to find the parts they needed.

They searched
The barn.
TOOLS

They searched the fields.

They searched
The pond.

They even searched
The junk yard!
Everywhere they looked, they found something new and exciting.

Finally, they found all the parts they needed to fix the flying saucer.

With a few adjustments
****ZIP! ZAP!****
and Zep's ship was
ready to fly.

Zep was so happy that he wanted to thank the boys for their help. He used his Martain powers to create a rainbow in the sky and a beautiful colorful Flower garden.

Oliver, Nathan
and baby
Landon were
amazed!

As Zep prepared to fly back home to Mars, and leave his new best friends.

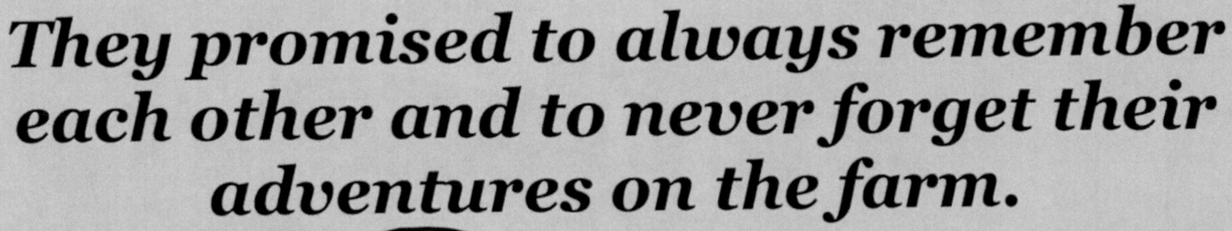

They promised to always remember each other and to never forget their adventures on the farm.

And so, Zep flew back to mars...

with a smile on his face and
a heart full of joy.

Zep may have been a silly little Martain, but he had learned a valuable lesson about the kindness and generosity of others. And he would always cherish the memories of his time on the farm with his new friends, Oliver, Nathan and baby Landon.

Made in United States
North Haven, CT
22 June 2023

38120968R00020